Behind AT THE ZOO

Adrienne B. Lieberman

Contents

Rigby

MAP LEGEND

Blue Trail
1. Penguins, Seabirds
2. Elephants, Giraffes
3. Bears, Wolves
4. Birds
5. Vultures, Eagles, Owls

Gold Trail
6. Monkeys
7. Lions, Tigers
8. Seals
9. Children's Zoo
10. Koala, Snakes, Bats
11. Swan Pond

Green Trail
12. Flamingos
13. Gorillas, Chimps
14. Zebras, Camels

Red Trail
15. Cows, Pigs, Horses

16—24. Rest Areas

We'll learn the answers to these questions and many others on a behind-the-scenes tour of Chicago's Lincoln Park Zoo. Not only will we see many animals up close, but we'll also get a chance to ask the zoo professionals questions about how they keep the animals' lives healthy, interesting, and fun.

McCormick Bird House

Before entering the service area at the back of each animal house, our guide, Lisa Taylor, reminds us to step on the footbath. This cleans the bottoms of our shoes and prevents us from tracking germs in and out.

The service area behind the bird exhibits holds stacks of trays and feeding bowls. Keeper Kim Garbacz studies a chart. It tells her what to feed the birds in each area. Next she weighs each meal carefully. A small room to the side of the service area contains cages for the crickets and mice that some birds eat.

Since the Bird House opens to the public at 10:00 A.M., the keepers hurry to get it ready. Each morning the keepers remove any uneaten food. They also scrub bird waste from the branches and the floors. Then they look for all the birds, checking their usual spots. All over the zoo, these jobs—cleaning, feeding, and checking the animals—take several hours at the start of each day.

Z**oo**ZONE!

QUESTION: How do you know what food and how much of it to give to the birds?

KEEPER KIM: A nutritionist studied the birds' diets. She had the keepers help her by writing down exactly what the birds ate and what they left behind. After her study, she advised the zookeepers exactly what to feed each bird. The jacanas, for example, used to eat only fish. Now they get insects, too.

QUESTION: How do you know how many birds to put in each area?

KEEPER KIM: We read books and articles to find out the normal population size for our space. Sometimes we simply try something to see if it works. If we put in ten birds and five keep flying out, we know we've put in too many.

9:15 A.M.
Lester Fisher Great Ape House

Today in the service area behind the gorilla habitat, keeper Roby Elsner is training Kwan, an eleven-year-old blackback gorilla. Before watching through a wide mesh screen, we'll need to put on masks. If we have a cold, we could pass it on to Kwan and the other gorillas, and we wouldn't want to do that.

Kwan has learned to show his hands, feet, and so on when asked. Training helps the keepers and veterinarians check sick animals more easily. It also helps the animals cooperate in necessary tasks, such as moving to another area or getting their nails clipped. Best of all, training keeps these intelligent animals lively and happy. Animals like gorillas and chimpanzees especially love learning new things.

Roby shows a small clicker. He clicks it each time his 330-pound student does what Roby asks. When he hears the click, Kwan knows he has earned a piece of fruit. Kwan has learned many things in the three years since he came to this zoo. Today Roby says, "Left shoulder," then presents a foot-long stick to the gorilla. Kwan eagerly touches his left shoulder to the stick. Roby

clicks and gives Kwan a grape. In turn, Kwan presents his right shoulder, his left and right arm, and each ear. He has also learned how to hold his mouth open wide. When we go to the front of the exhibit and put our hand up to the thick glass, Roby gives Kwan a signal from across the room. Kwan quickly shows the behavior Roby taught him to perform for a scene in a recent movie—he puts his hand right up to ours.

ZOO ZONE!

QUESTION: How did you train Kwan to let you clip his nails?

KEEPER ROBY: It took two weeks with two lessons each day. With each lesson I added something new to a behavior he already knew. First I taught him to show each finger to me. Then I rewarded him when he let me touch each finger lightly with the clippers. Next, I slowly added pressure with the clippers. After I clipped a little bit, I gave him two bananas. That was a bonus jackpot. Finally, he let me clip all his nails.

Kwan is my best student. He could easily hurt me, but all our hours of training have built a strong bond between us.

ZOO ZONE!

QUESTION: How do keepers train most animals?

KEEPER ROBY: Food works well to reward animals. Almost all of our training is done with food rewards.

QUESTION: What makes an animal easier or harder to train?

KEEPER ROBY: Very curious animals are easier to train because they like to try new things. The golden-headed lion tamarins in the Small Mammal House are curious, but they are also very shy. The loudness of the clicker startled them. It took more than two months to get them used to it. We used a quieter clicker to train the tiny mouse lemurs. They also found the loud sound frightening.

11:30 A.M.
Searle Animal Hospital

Dr. Natalie Mylniczenko, one of the zoo's veterinarians, is getting ready to send a two-year-old iguana back to the Children's Zoo. One of the keepers had reported that this lizard had stopped eating.

"We checked her," says the veterinarian. "Her belly felt very full." In fact, the iguana was full of eggs. They could be seen on a special picture called an *ultrasound*. Her behavior was perfectly normal, the vet explains. "When iguanas are about to lay eggs, they normally stop eating."

The keepers at the Children's Zoo will give her a special covered nest where she can lay her eggs.

ZOO ZONE!

QUESTION: Do the animals act differently toward you because of your job?

DR. NATALIE: Some know me as the vet that gives them shots. That can make them aggressive. One of the lions roars loudly every time she sees me. She's used to her keepers, but she doesn't like the vets. Even so, animals can also be very forgiving. Recently I had to give a female gorilla named Debbie a drug she didn't like. When Debbie was waking up, she punched the door of her cage at me. It was like she was saying, "How could you do this to me?" But later she played with me to show me she wasn't angry anymore. Whenever I have time, I always go in and feed them grapes. That way they won't hate me if I need to give them a shot.

QUESTION: How do you get sick animals to take their food or medicine?

DR. NATALIE: That can be a challenge. For a while a big baboon called a *mandrill* wanted to eat only fruit. To feed him a normal diet that includes grains, vegetables, and vitamins, we had to grind this food and bake it into blueberry muffins. For a while he was eating three or four of those muffins a day. Now he is down to just one muffin a day in addition to his regular diet. We sometimes have to hide medicine in the fish or mice that birds and snakes eat. A sick snake might even get a mouse milkshake. That's a liquid diet with a mouse blended in.

ZooZONE!

QUESTION: How can you tell an animal is sick?

DR. NATALIE: We depend on the keepers, who see the animals every day. They tell us if an animal is behaving differently. Another sign is that a sick animal will eat less or lose weight. To examine a sick lion or tiger, we have to give it a shot to put it to sleep for a little while. But some of our animals—the gorillas, elephants, and rhinos, for example—have been trained to cooperate during a checkup.

1:00 P.M.
Kovler Lion House

Cindy Swisher, the lead keeper in the service area of the Lion House, makes sure a big blue barrel that's been in the lion's habitat has been cleaned properly. After cleaning and checking it, the keepers will put it into the jaguars' exhibit. One end of the barrel is torn. The torn edge shows how popular this item is with the wild cats. Outside the zoo they would have to stalk and catch their own food. The blue barrel, called an *enrichment item*, helps keep those skills alive. The cats eagerly pounce on the barrel, bounce it, and bat it around. Moving it from exhibit to exhibit prevents the animals from getting bored with it.

In the zoo, the cats eat a scientific diet of ground meat with vitamins. Twice a week they get a treat: meat on the bone. One day each week the big cats get nothing at all to eat. That is because in the wild they would not eat every day. Each morning they go to holding areas. There they eat while their living areas get cleaned.

ZOO ZONE!

QUESTION: How do keepers safely move lions, tigers, and other large cats to their holding areas for feeding or medical care?

KEEPER CINDY: The animals are trained to move into the holding areas with the reward of a meatball. If they don't come in, we simply try again later. For medical care, we may use a squeeze cage that can be connected to the holding area. We train the animals to enter the squeeze cage with a food reward. This cage has two special features. It contains a scale so we can see how much a cat weighs. It also has a movable panel. The panel holds the cat snugly enough to allow an exam by a keeper or veterinarian.

ZOO ZONE!

QUESTION: Is it dangerous to handle these large cats?

KEEPER CINDY: It can be. That's why safety is our number-one goal for the animals, the keepers, and the visitors. People who work in the zoo learn to ask themselves basic safety questions and follow the rules carefully each time. In the service area, a large sign warns keepers to double-check locks and to inspect all doors before moving the cats.

QUESTION: How can you tell which enrichment items—like the blue barrel—different animals like?

ARE ALL YOUR LOCKS LOCKED?

KEEPER CINDY: On a calendar we note the animal's reaction on a 1-to-5 scale:

1—No reaction

2—Scared of/Avoid

3—Look at/No interaction

4—Some interaction (less than 5 minutes)

5—Much interaction (more than 5 minutes and repeated throughout the day)

If an animal does not play with an item that we have tried two or three times, we may try changing it or we will drop it from the list. If an animal avoids or is overly scared of an item more than once, we will not offer it again.

2:45 P.M.
Regenstein Small Mammal-Reptile House

Dave Bernier, the lead keeper in the Small Mammal-Reptile House, has just heard some bad news. He is responsible for the well-being of PB, the twenty-one-year-old koala. Because of a snowstorm in Chicago, the plane carrying PB's usual food—eucalyptus leaves—is stuck on the ground in Florida. Eucalyptus trees grow in tropical climates. Fresh leaves are shipped twice a week to the zoo. PB weighs only about 15 pounds, but because her food comes from so far away, it costs more to feed her than it does to feed an elephant.

The people who run the zoo are prepared for such emergencies. In a greenhouse at the zoo, gardeners raise some eucalyptus plants. Luckily, they have stored a three-day supply of the tasty leaves in the refrigerator. PB will have plenty to eat, despite the blizzard.

In addition to small mammals like PB, cold-blooded reptiles also live in this house. Like PB, they also require special food and a carefully controlled environment. Each snake has a box that is set to just the right temperature. Keepers change the temperature to match the seasons of the animal's natural habitat.

ZOOZONE!

QUESTION: How are temperature and light adjusted for the comfort of small mammals?

KEEPER DAVE: The koala is the most sensitive mammal in this habitat. That's why the sensors for temperature and light are next to the koala's area. These sensors trigger a computer program. It can automatically turn the lights on or off, open or close the shades, and open or close the windows—all for PB's health and comfort.

QUESTION: How do you move a snake safely?

KEEPER DAVE: We use long-handled hooks. You can hook a snake and drop it into a tall barrel to feed it or move it to the hospital for treatment.

QUESTION: What do you feed the frogs and snakes?

KEEPER DAVE: Frogs eat tiny pinhead crickets. Most snakes eat mice. Different-sized snakes are fed different-sized mice.

5:00 P.M.
McCormick Bird House

In the daily log, Kim finishes writing her notes on the birds' behaviors before going home for the night. In a date book, she records another important piece of information. One bird has begun to sit on an egg. On the date 21 days later, she makes another entry. That note will remind her to watch for the results. She hopes to see a baby bird hatch.

QUESTION: How do keepers in the Bird House tell the birds apart to make notes on them?

KEEPER KIM: The bigger birds, such as the toucans and the frogmouths, look different from one another. Smaller birds are identified by their leg bands. Males get banded on the right leg, and females wear bands on the left leg.

ZOOZONE!

QUESTION: Why does one bird attack another?

KEEPER KIM: Like other animals, birds act to protect their territory. Today one of the jacanas threatened a smaller bird called a stilt. The jacana may have behaved this way because the stilt was new to the exhibit. We write down a description of this behavior in our log book. That reminds all the keepers to watch the jacana closely.

10:00 P.M.
The Farm-in-the-Zoo

Pam Jackson, one of the zoo's night keepers, has just finished milking the dairy's cows and goats at the farm in the zoo. Pam makes rounds through different parts of the zoo. Nothing unusual has happened tonight. But one night recently someone reported seeing a sick flamingo. Pam helped take the flamingo to the animal hospital. There, Dr. Natalie warmed the flamingo and gave her fluids until she recovered.

Pam continues to make her rounds. At each animal house, she will fill out a report to be read by the day keepers the next morning. In just a few hours the day keepers will be back to start their next day's work.

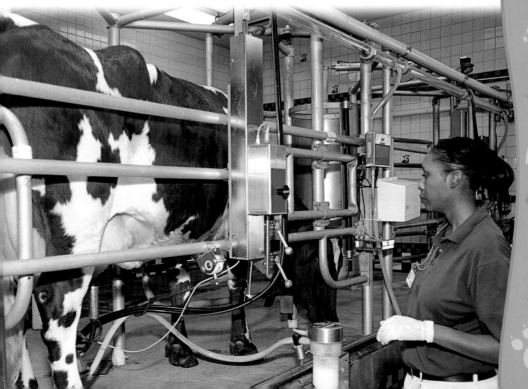

WHO'S WHO in the ZOO

Job title	Duties
keeper	• cleans habitats • prepares food, feeds animals, and helps plan diets • trains and plans enrichment activities for the animals
lead keeper	• does the same things that other keepers do • plans the other keepers' work schedules • lets the veterinarian know if an animal is sick, and helps secure a sick animal for a checkup
veterinarian	• cares for sick animals • does regular checkups and gives animals shots to keep them healthy • helps plan the animals' diets

Enrichment

Stalking the blue barrel in the Lion House and other enrichment activities let animals act as they would in the wild. At Lincoln Park Zoo, the keepers and the veterinarians made a long list of enrichment activities that are safe and fun for different animals. Then they divided these activities into types:

Type 1	**Food**	This includes new kinds of approved food and different ways to offer it to the animals.
Type 2	**Scent**	This includes any kind of smell, such as the scent of a hunted animal.
Type 3	**Other**	This includes things like the blue barrel for the wild cats or tapes of different sounds.

Instead of rotating the types of enrichment activities in the same order each week, the keepers schedule these activities at random. Here is a typical calendar for a week.

Sunday	Monday	Tuesday	Wednesday	Thursday	Friday	Saturday
Type 1 ①	Type 2 ②	Type 3 ③	Type 1 ④	Keeper's Choice ⑤	Type 3 ⑥	Type 2 ⑦

INDEX